F. Ethel Hynam

The Secrets of the Night

and other Esthonian Tales

F. Ethel Hynam

The Secrets of the Night
and other Esthonian Tales

ISBN/EAN: 9783337082413

Printed in Europe, USA, Canada, Australia, Japan

Cover: Foto ©Andreas Hilbeck / pixelio.de

More available books at **www.hansebooks.com**

THE EUROPEAN FOLK TALE SERIES.

THE

SECRETS OF THE NIGHT,

AND OTHER

ESTHONIAN TALES.

TRANSLATED BY

F. ETHEL HYNAM.

ILLUSTRATED BY H. OAKES-JONES.

LONDON :

ELLIOT STOCK, 62, PATERNOSTER ROW, E.C.

1899.

THE revival of interest in folk-lore and fairy tales is one of the most marked and, at the same time, encouraging incidents in modern literature.

Some few years ago these works were only known to the few—were hardly classed as books by the critics or by the public; now they are valued by the one, and eagerly looked for by the other. The remote by-ways of tradition are being examined for examples of these tales, and every land and every language brought under tribute to supply the new demand.

Hitherto, however, no systematic attempt seems to have been made to gather together into one series a representative selection of Fairy Tales of other lands. The EUROPEAN FOLK-TALE SERIES is an attempt to do this, and, while avoiding the known or hackneyed, to give characteristic examples of each land, racy of the soil, and peculiar to the people.

The tales are, for the most part, now first presented to the world in an English garb. When complete, the publisher believes that a representative and catholic collection of little known and yet valuable legends will be within the reach of the reader. The series will be complete in about twelve volumes, representing, amongst others, the Esthonian, Russian, Mongolian, Slavonic, Polish, Bohemian, Servian, Magyar, and Scandinavian races.

The present volume deals with Esthonian, perhaps one of the least known branches of the great Folklore family. Up to a few years ago very little was known of Esthonian tales. One or two might be met with here and there in large collections, but it was not until Dr. Kreutzwald edited them that any real attempt was made to collect them in any number. Speaking of the characteristics of these stories it has been well said : ' Many signs show unmistakably a Lithuanian source, or, at least, contact; others, more recent, indicate Russian origin. As the coast of Esthonia and the adjacent islands had a Swedish population, there are borrowed from them many stories as well as many myths springing from the earliest times. Others, more modern, show German traces and characteristics of dwellers in towns as well as the country.' Over sixty examples of Esthonian folk-lore have been collected, edited, and published under the auspices of the Finnish Literary Society. These are, of course, of varying merit. The present volume presents to the English reader what the translator believes to be the best and most marked of the collection. No attempt has been made to alter the styles of these tales; on the contrary, the aim has been to present them to the reader as closely in their native garb as the exigencies of our language will permit. Artistic feeling and no small amount of poetry will be found in most of these stories, and while there is no lack of magic and witchcraft, dragons, serpents, and other monsters, still it appears to the translator that the construction of the stories shows a skill that interests the reader apart from these attractions, and will, it is hoped, make the first volume, 'The Secrets of the Night, and other Esthonian Tales,' acceptable to the public in general, and to the folk-lore student in particular.

CONTENTS

	PAGE
THE SECRETS OF THE NIGHT	11
THE SUBTERRANEAN KINGDOM	25
THE MERMAID	39
FORTUNE'S EGG	57
THE NORTHLAND DRAGON	71
TONTLA FOREST	91

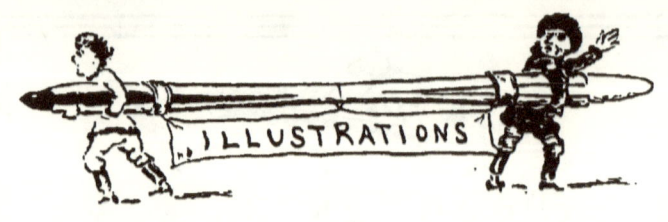

ILLUSTRATIONS

EUROPEAN FOLK-TALE SERIES - - *Frontispiece*

PREFACE - - - - - - *Page* v

CONTENTS - - - - - ,, ix

ILLUSTRATIONS - - - - - ,, x

VIGNETTE TO 'SECRETS OF THE NIGHT' - - ,, 12

THEY DANCED ROUND THE MARBLE BASIN - - ,, 19

TAILPIECE - - - - - - ,, 24

HANS FINDS THE ENTRANCE TO THE CAVERN - ,, 26

LED HANS TO WHERE THE MID-DAY REPAST WAS

    LAID · - - - - - ,, 34

TAILPIECE - - - - - ,, 37

VIGNETTE TO 'THE MERMAID' - - - ,, 40

THE MERMAID COMES BACK TO SLEEPY TÖNNIS - ,, 46

TAILPIECE - - - - - ,, 55

VIGNETTE TO 'FORTUNE'S EGG' - - - ,, 58

SHE FELL AT HIS FEET AND WEPT BITTERLY - ,, 66

TAILPIECE - - - - - ,, 69

VIGNETTE TO 'THE NORTHLAND DRAGON' - - ,, 72

'THIS IS MY DEAREST TREASURE,' SHE SAID - ,, 80

TAILPIECE - - - - - ,, 90

TONTLA FOREST - - - - - ,, 92

'FORM ME AN IMITATION OF THIS MAIDEN' - ,, 101

TAILPIECE - - - - - ,, 110

THE SECRETS OF THE NIGHT.

AR, far away in a small village in the cold and dreary province of Finland there lived, many years ago, a young peasant. He was very poor, and had to toil hard all day long cultivating the unfruitful soil. But in spite of poverty and hard work, he was always cheerful, for he was strong and healthy, and had few wants, though it must be confessed that sometimes life seemed to him very hard. Finland being but thinly peopled, our young peasant lived much alone, but this solitude did not trouble him in the least; he loved to be alone with Nature, to muse on all her wonders, and study her many changes. As he guided his oxen at their work, and strove to make the furrows sufficiently deep, he would often pause in his labour to watch the lark as it rose from its nest on the dewy ground, and mounted in triumphant freedom high above the morning cloud, warbling its exulting lay, that swelled ever louder and louder the nearer it approached the sky. And as he listened to its notes of sweetest ecstasy, they

seemed to awaken an answering echo within his breast, and to bear his soul away with them, far above earthly things; and when at length the lark was lost to view, and its song had died away in the far distance, he would resume his work with a lighter heart and renewed courage.

The village in which this peasant lived was surrounded by large and gloomy forests; indeed, the greater part of the country is covered with forests so vast that it has been said that to wander through them is much like wandering over the bottom of some mighty ocean. During the summer, so short in the northern regions, the air is unusually clear, and then our hero could see far away in the distance the large lakes, which in Finland are very numerous, glittering like mirrors among the forest trees. As the weary day turned to his rest, and evening, wrapped in her mantle of gray, stole softly on, touching all things with her opiate wand, and casting her soft veil over the eyes of day without causing their light to entirely disappear, he felt, as it were, an excess of vital energy that all the hard labour of the day had been unable to exhaust. As the darkness increased, this feeling changed to a strange wild longing after the unknown. Then as he gazed forth into the gloom, the trees waving their long arms to and fro seemed to beckon him, and the voices of the night to summon him; and he would wander far away into the forest in pursuit of the weird shadows that crept among the trees, and flying ever before him, seemed to shrink together as he approached.

' In this strange twilight,' thought he, ' the secrets
of the night must surely hide'; and these mysteries
he desired beyond all things to know.

Unable at length to longer resist his desire to
understand the hidden workings of Nature, the
young peasant sought a magician, or, to give him
his proper Esthonian name, a Mana-Berehrer, who
from time to time visited the village, told him of his
wish, and asked his aid.

' It might perhaps be done,' said the magician
after a few moments' consideration. ' But think the
matter well over, for I warn you, it will bring you no
happiness.'

But the peasant paid no heed to the old man's
warning, and persisted in his desire.

' Well then, have your own way,' replied the
magician. ' Take this piece of bread and preserve
it carefully. On Midsummer's Eve the king of the
serpents assembles his legions on the borders of
the forest, and drinks the milk of snipe out of a
golden shell. Should you succeed in dipping that
piece of bread into the shell and then swallow it
quickly, you will gain the knowledge you desire.
But I warn you once more you had much better
leave it alone.'

Though it wanted but a few days to midsummer
the time of waiting seemed endless to the poor
peasant. With the decline of each day his longings
after the unknown increased; he cared nothing for
the magician's warning.

The night so ardently desired at length arrived,
and he hastened to the stretch of meadow that

bordered the forest. There in the centre of the field
he saw to his astonishment a small mound that
certainly had not been there earlier in the day.
Suddenly a bright light shone forth over the hill, and
from every side he heard a strange sound of hissing
and rushing; all around him darted adders, vipers
and serpents, both large and small, all moving rapidly
towards the hill, which grew gradually larger and
larger. Urged on by an irresistible impulse, he
followed them, and found that what he had taken
for a hill was in reality an enormous crowd of serpents. In the centre of this vast throng was a huge
serpent, thick as the thickest fir-tree, reared aloft on
his tail, whilst the others coiled themselves in rings
around his gigantic body, their eyes flaming and
glittering like living coals. The centre serpent reared
himself ever higher and higher, waving his great
head to and fro; on it he wore a golden crown from
which there streamed forth innumerable rays of
dazzling light, and by this the peasant knew he must
be the serpent king. Suddenly the huge monster
shot forth his long fiery tongue, and our poor hero
grew stiff with terror, but the next moment his
courage revived, for there, straight before his eyes,
was the golden shell filled with milk. Stretching
forth his hand, he dipped his piece of bread into the
shell, and then quickly swallowed it. He had no
sooner done this than the hissing and rushing
increased a hundredfold, and he fled from the spot,
terror lending wings to his feet, and he had a feeling
that he came from that place much quicker than at
any previous time. On and on he sped until at

length, his strength failing, he sank exhausted on the ground. When he recovered consciousness it was broad daylight ; he was far away from the scene of his adventure, and after his rest felt quite strong and cheerful. It was the snipe's milk that had given him this strength, and he now waited until it should make his power of vision clear.

As the sun sank slowly to his rest, shedding his parting smile over the earth, and evening casting her placid shades over the scene veiled the landscape with her gentle touch, he hastened forth into the forest, and by the time the slight darkness of the night cast her sombre mantle over the earth he had reached an open space surrounded by birch-trees, whose silver stems glistened in the pale moonlight. He had often visited this spot before, but to-night it was strangely changed. Instead of the soft marshy ground, he beheld a round enclosure built of polished marble of a golden hue, adorned with the most exquisite workmanship, and filled with water clear as crystal ; it looked like a bath of unusual dimensions. Full of curiosity, he carefully concealed himself behind a tree to wait for what might occur. About midnight light misty forms began to emerge from among the trees on every side. They were all maidens of the most rare beauty, clad in robes of light, floating gauze, the whiteness of which in some changed to a greenish, in others to a bluish hue, and in their hair they wore precious stones, blue and green, which sent forth a dazzling radiance. As soon as they reached the marble basin they cast aside their light garments and descended into the

2

water, from which they almost immediately emerged. This action they repeated many times, until at length the bath was ended. Then all the maidens formed in a circle and danced round and round the marble basin with undulating and irregular, but still very graceful, movements. Their long hair fell in floating masses around their slender forms; not a breath of air stirred the foliage, nor was there a sound to be heard. On the borders of the forest far away to the west a few faintly-glowing streaks still lingered, showing where the sun had sunk to his rest, whilst a deep red tinge in the clouds in the east already marked the part where he would rise again in his splendour. At the same time the moon, encircled with a zone of soft and tender light, shed her gentle rays through the branches of the birch-trees. The young man's heart beat fast, and his temples throbbed; he remained motionless, scarcely daring to breathe for fear of disturbing the lovely dancers. As the mysterious twilight grew clearer, a mist he had not hitherto observed spread gradually over the scene, becoming ever thicker and whiter, yet still the swiftly-moving forms were indistinctly visible. But when the first flickering rays of morning penetrated the gloom of the forest every trace of the lovely vision had disappeared, lost in the impenetrable mist.

The young man then came forth from his hiding-place, and passed again over the open ground. He was not long in so doing, but the water of the marsh filled his shoes, for the marble basin had disappeared, and the ground had resumed its wonted appearance.

HEY DANCED ROUND THE MARBLE BASIN.

2—2

When he reached home he threw himself, exhausted, on his bed, and fell into a light, half-waking slumber ; but even during sleep this one joy absorbed his mind : he now knew what no other mortal had ever yet known, and had seen that which human eye had never before beheld. When he awoke this feeling became more intense, filling his whole soul with an indescribable pleasure, but this was now mixed with an impatient longing for the arrival of night. It came at length, and he hastened once more into the forest, and there, from his hiding-place among the trees, beheld again the lovely vision that had so enraptured him on the preceding night ; on the third night the same scene met his view, and his joy almost overpowered him.

The fourth night found him again at the open space in the forest. The pale moon looked down from her silent throne, bathing all things in a flood of silver light ; the white stems of the birch-trees bent as usual towards the grass ; the mist was slowly rising. It was a most lovely spot. But the beauty of the scene had no charms for our hero ; his thoughts were full of the beauteous maidens, and he anxiously awaited their reappearance. But he waited in vain ; they did not come, though he watched the whole night through. Then, after wandering for some time aimlessly through the forest, he returned home sorrowful and discontented. The same bitter disappointment met him the next night, and on every succeeding night. For a whole week he sought the open space in the forest in the vain hope of gazing once again on the enchanting scene. Then he sought out other places, observant of the slightest thing that seemed to indicate the reappearance of the beauteous maidens who now filled his every thought; but all his wanderings were in vain.

Each night was spent in fruitless search after the longed-for vision. His work was neglected, all real objects repulsed his mind; there was nothing that now awoke in him either anticipation or remonstrance. Through the snipe's milk he had taken he understood every movement of the shadows, and could clearly distinguish each one of those indistinct sounds so numerous in the forest. But this, far from giving him pleasure, caused him the greatest uneasiness.

His misery was very great, and to escape from it he sought the summer feast held every year in the district. To this feast the scattered population flocked from far and near, and our young peasant with the rest; he had never avoided the men, and had always been glad to meet the maidens, though his heart was not given to any. But this feast, which had formerly given him such pleasure, was now only a fresh cause of grief; it seemed as though he had come there from another sphere of life, and found his surroundings very different to those among which he had grown up. The unnatural clearness with which his mind was now gifted in regard to the things of Nature remained with him in his sojourn among men. It presented to his view many tokens of unfairness, many deformed ideas of the hardships and necessities of life, and these for the first time weighed heavily on his mind, and the joy of the assembly seemed to him only discontent and discord. He experienced a feeling of anger and envy because no one saw things with the same refined clearness as himself; the feast became unbearable to him, and he began anew his wanderings in the solitude of the forest.

At length the thought occurred to him that, as he now saw what formerly he had only feebly imagined, and knew clearly what before had only worked dimly within him, his daily work would be lighter and more pleasant; but when he began to put the idea into practice he found his work none the less an intolerable burden, and the beauty of the day that he used to regard as a promise from heaven was now only a mockery. His soul was full of painful memories, and his anguish increased daily.

At length one morning he went into the forest to seek out the magician. The old man was clad in his travelling dress, a staff was in his hand and he was just setting forth on a journey to another village. The peasant stopped him and told him of his distress.

' Then your wish has really been fulfilled,' replied the magician, ' and my art has been proved. You have learned the most hidden secret of the Esthonian night. You have been highly favoured, for to you it has been permitted to watch the assembling of the daughters Mets-hallias and Muru-eides, the goddesses of earth and water. On their alliance the fruitfulness of the earth depends, and they renew it in this forest with bathing and dances.'

' Will they come again ? Shall I yet once again behold them ?' cried the young man, with sparkling eyes. ' I would endure years of misery only to see those beauteous forms once more.'

' They assemble for three successive nights at midsummer every hundred years,' replied the magician. ' I have just told you that what you saw is one of the strangest and most hidden of all the secrets of night. But a repetition of that entrancing sight you cannot live to see.'

The young man gazed at him wildly for a few moments, and then exclaimed in accents of despair :

' It was cruel, it was wicked of you not to tell me this ! Nothing now remains for me but endless misery !'

' Consider for a moment. Would it have been of any use ?' replied the magician, turning away.

The peasant made a sudden movement as though he would have sprung on him, but sank back, half-fainting, against a tree. There he sat, half-dazed, amidst the luxuriance of the day, as midst the ruins of a fallen house, dismayed at the thought that he was still compelled to live. At length he was found by the inhabitants of the place, who took him home, and for some time his life was despaired of. Though he recovered, thoughts of the beauteous vision he might never again behold were ever present with him, filling his soul with misery and despair. Day after day he wandered listlessly through the forest, longing in vain to anticipate time, and calling wildly on death to release him from his misery. His cry was heard, he began to look old, and he wasted away visibly, and at the end of a few years Death summoned him from the scene of his sufferings. His sad story was then made known, and all who knew him rejoiced that his sorrows were at length ended.

THE SUBTERRANEAN KINGDOM.

HANS FINDS THE ENTRANCE TO THE CAVERN.

NE stormy night, between Christmas and the New Year, a peasant missed his road whilst trying to force his way through some deep snow-drifts. His strength failed, and he blessed his good fortune when he at length found a shelter from the wind beneath a thick juniper-tree. Here he determined to pass the night, hoping to find his way more easily by the light of morning. He drew his limbs together like a hedgehog, wrapped himself in his warm fur coat, and soon fell asleep. I know not how long he had lain thus when he felt some one shaking him. As he started from his sleep a strange voice sounded in his ear :

'Peasant, awake! Stand up, otherwise you will be buried in the snow and unable to get out !'

The sleeper pushed his head out of his fur coat and opened wide his eyes, still stupid with sleep. There before him stood a man of tall though slender stature, who carried as a stick a young fir-tree double the height of the bearer.

'Come with me,' said the man with the fir-tree

stick; 'a fire is waiting for us beneath the trees in
the forest, where we can rest better than out here in
the open country.'

The man could not refuse such a kind invitation;
he stood up at once, and stepped briskly forward
with the stranger. The snowstorm raged around
them so furiously it was impossible to see three steps
in advance; but when the stranger raised his fir-tree
staff, and cried with a loud voice, ' Ho, ho ! Mother
of the storm, make room !' immediately there opened
before them a wide path whereon no snowflake fell.
On either side and behind them the snowstorm
raged in all its fury, but the wanderer felt it not. It
was as though on both sides an invisible wand kept
back the storm. Soon they came to the forest, from
which, while yet afar off, the bright light of a fire
shone towards them.

' What is your name ?' asked the man with the
fir-tree stick, and the peasant replied :

' Hans, the son of Long Hans.'

Beside the fire sat three men clad in white linen
garments, as though it were the middle of summer.
Moreover, for a circle of about thirty feet or more,
summer beauty reigned : the moss was dry, plants
flourished, and the grass swarmed with ants and
beetles. From afar off, however, the son of Long
Hans still heard the rush of snow and the roaring of
the wind. Yet more wonderful than aught beside
was the fire, which burned brightly and shed forth a
cheerful radiance without raising the least cloud of
smoke.

' What think you, son of Long Hans ; is not this

a better resting-place in which to pass the night than out yonder in the open country, beneath the juniper-tree?'

To this Hans agreed, and again thanked the stranger for so kindly bringing him to a place of shelter. Then he threw off his fur coat, rolled it into a pillow for his head, and lay down to rest beside the glowing fire. The man with the fir-tree stick took a small barrel from out the thicket, and offered Hans a refreshing draught that tasted excellent, then he likewise stretched himself on the ground, and began to talk with his companions in a strange language, of which our Hans could not understand one single word. He therefore soon fell asleep.

When he awoke he was alone in a strange place, where there was no longer either forest or fire. He rubbed his eyes, and recalled the events of the past night. He thought he must have dreamt it all. Still, he could not understand, if this were really the case, how he had come hither to a place that was quite strange to him. Then from afar a loud noise broke on his ear, and he felt the earth tremble beneath his feet. Hans listened for some time to ascertain whence the noise proceeded, and then resolved to journey in that direction, hoping to meet some human being.

Following the sound, he came at length to the mouth of a rocky cavern, in which a bright fire was burning. He entered, and found himself in an enormous smithy, with innumerable forge-bellows and anvils. At each anvil stood seven workers. More curious smiths could not have been found in

the whole world.   The little men, who only reached
to the knee of an ordinary man, had beards longer
than their tiny bodies, and wielded hammers more
than twice their own size.   But they gave such
mighty blows on the anvil with their heavy iron
clubs, that the strongest men could not have dealt
more powerful blows.   For clothing these little men
wore leather aprons, reaching from their necks to
their feet.

On a large block of iron beside the further wall
sat Hans' friend, the old man with the fir-tree stick,
keeping a sharp look-out on the work of the little
company.   At his feet stood a large tankard, from
which the workers took an occasional draught.   The
Lord of the Smiths no longer wore the white garments of yesterday; instead, he had on a black
Russian coat, whilst a leather girdle with an enormous clasp encircled his waist.   With his fir-tree
stick he from time to time signed to the workers—in
such a noise to speak would have been useless.

Hans was not certain if anyone had noticed him,
since master and servants continued their work
without heeding the arrival of the stranger.   After a
few hours the little smiths were allowed a rest; the
bellows were stopped, and the heavy hammers
thrown on the ground.   As the workers left the
cavern, the host rose from his seat, called Hans to
him, and said:

' I noticed your entrance, but, as the work pressed,
I could not speak with you sooner.   To-day you
must be my guest, and learn to know my house-
keeping and manner of living.   Amuse yourself

here for a time, whilst I lay aside these black garments.'

With these words he drew a key from his pocket, unlocked a door in the wall of the cavern, and bade Hans enter.

Oh, what treasures and riches Hans beheld here! Bars of silver and of gold piled all round glittered and sparkled before his eyes. Hans tried to count the bars of gold in one of the heaps, and had just reached five hundred and fifty when his host returned, and exclaimed, laughing:

'Leave the counting alone—it will take too much time. Instead, take a few bars from the heap. I will give you them as a remembrance.'

Naturally, Hans did not require to be told twice. With both hands he seized a bar of gold, but found to his distress he was unable to stir it from its place, to say nothing of raising it. His host laughed and said:

'You puny creature! you are unable to take away the smallest of my presents. Content yourself, therefore, with the pleasure of beholding them.'

So saying, he led Hans into another room, from thence into a third, a fourth, and so on until they entered the seventh. This was large as a large church, and, like the others, filled from floor to roof with piles of gold and silver.

Hans marvelled greatly at these innumerable treasures, sufficient to have purchased all the kingdoms of the world, but which lay here useless beneath the earth. He asked his host:

'Wherefore do you heap up such an enormous

treasure, if no living being derives any benefit from all the gold and silver? If this treasure came into the hands of men, they would all become rich: no one would need to work, no one would suffer want.'

'It is just for that reason,' replied the host, 'that I dare not deliver this treasure to mankind; the whole world would go to rack and ruin through idleness, if man no longer needed to earn his daily bread. Man is created to support himself through toil and care.'

Hans then asked his host to explain the use of having all the gold and silver lying glittering here, the possessions of one man, and why the Lord of the Gold should unceasingly strive to increase his treasure when he already had such an abundance. The old man made reply:

'I am no mortal man, though I have the like form and features. I am one of those higher beings formed by the Creator to manage the world. By his command I with my little company must, without ceasing, form gold and silver here under the earth; a small part of this is given out every year for the use of men, but scarcely so much as they need to carry on their business. But no one may possess the gift without trouble. We must therefore first beat the gold very fine, and then mix the grains with earth, clay and sand; later they will be found in this granite where fortune wills, and must be sought for carefully. But now, my friend, we must break off our conversation, for the dinner-hour approaches. If you desire to examine my treasures further, remain here and rejoice your heart with the glitter of gold until I return to summon you to dinner.'

With this he departed and Hans was left alone.

Hans moved restlessly from one treasure-chamber to the other, trying here and there to lift just a very small piece of gold, but in vain. He had often heard clever people say how heavy gold was, but he never believed it—now he learned it by experience. After a time his host returned, but so changed that at the first glance Hans did not recognise him. He was clad in flame-coloured silk garments, richly embroidered in gold and with a gold fringe; a broad girdle of gold encircled his waist, and on his head glittered a golden crown, from which innumerable precious stones sparkled like stars on a bright winter's night. Instead of the fir-tree stick, he held a small wand wrought of fine gold, which possessed such ramifications that it looked like a shoot of the fir-tree stick.

When the lord of all this wealth had locked the doors of his treasure chambers and put the key carefully in his pocket, he took Hans by the hand and led him through the smiths' workshop into another apartment where the mid-day repast was prepared. In the centre of the room was a beautiful silver dining-table, and on either side of it a silver chair. The vessels for eating and drinking, the bowls, dishes, plates, tankards and cups, were of pure gold. When Hans and his host were seated at the table, twelve dishes were brought in one after the other; the servants were just like the little men in the smithy, except that they wore clean shining

LED HANS TO WHERE THE MID-DAY REPAST WAS LAID.

garments. Very wonderful to Hans was their swiftness and dexterity, for although no wings were
visible, they moved to and fro as lightly as though
they really had feathers. Not being tall enough to
reach, they were obliged to hop like flies from the
floor to the table. At the same time they held
large and small dishes filled with various meats in
their hands, and had to take care that no drop was
spilled. During the repast the little servants poured
mead and costly wines from the tankards into the
cups, and handed them to the feasters. The host
conversed kindly and explained to Hans various
secrets. Therefore when the conversation turned
on his night-meeting with Hans, he said :

'Between Christmas and the New Year I often
wander about the world for pleasure, to observe the
doings of men and to learn to know a few of them.
I cannot greatly praise what I have seen and known
of them up to the present. The greater number of
men live to injure and annoy one another. Each
complains more or less of the other. None see
their own mistakes and guilt, but condemn in others
the faults they themselves have committed.'

Hans strove as best he could to disprove the truth
of these words, but the kindly host caused him to
be so plenteously supplied with wine that at length
his tongue became so heavy he could not utter a
single word, and moreover was unable to understand what his host said to him. In short, he slept
in his chair.

During his sleep he dreamed a wonderful dream,
in which the golden bars passed continually before

him. He felt himself growing stronger and stronger,
and taking a couple of the gold bars on his back he
bore them away with ease. At length his strength
gave way beneath his heavy burden, and he was
obliged to sit down and take breath. He heard the
sound of merry voices, and thought it was the song
of the little smiths, then the bright fire from the
forge flashed before his eyes. He looked up blink-
ing, and found he was lying on the soft grass in the
green forest, there was no fire from the forge, but
only the rays of the sun looking kindly in his face.
He now tore himself fully from the bands of sleep, but
it was long ere he could recall what had occurred.

When his senses were again on the alert, all
appeared to him so strange and wonderful that he
knew not how to reconcile it with the natural order
of things. Hans remembered having lost his way
one stormy night shortly after Christmas, then all
that had befallen him later arose again in his
memory. He had spent the night by the fire with
a strange man who carried a fir-tree stick, had
passed the next day as guest of this same stranger,
had stayed to dinner with him, and drunk a good
deal ; in short, he had spent two days in revelling
and feasting. Looking around, he found himself
in the neighbourhood of an old fireplace, that
glittered brightly in the sun, and on examining the
place more closely he discovered that the supposed
ashes were really fine silver, and that the firebrands
still remaining were pure gold. Oh, what happiness ! But where to obtain a sack to carry the
treasure home ? Necessity is full of devices. Taking

off his winter coat, Hans swept the silver ashes into
a heap, being careful to leave none behind, put them
and the gold brands into the coat, and then tied the
corners together with his girdle, so that nothing
could fall out. Although the burden was not large, it
was so heavy that he was almost exhausted before he
found a suitable place wherein to conceal his treasure.

In this strange manner did Hans suddenly become
a rich man, rich enough to have bought a large
estate. But when he thought the matter over, he
considered it best to leave his old dwelling-place,
and go far away to a region where he was unknown.
There he bought a nice property, and had a good
sum of money still remaining. Then he took a
wife, and lived happily as a rich man to the end of
his days. Before his death he told his children
the story of how his subterranean host had made
him a rich man. And by the mouths of his children
and his children's children the story has been handed
down unto this day.

THE MERMAID.

THE MERMAID.

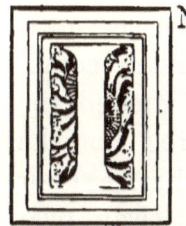N the happy olden days men were much better than they are now, therefore Heaven permitted them to behold many wonders which to-day are invisible, or but rarely appear to some favourite of fortune. True it is the birds sing after the old manner, and the animals still exchange their ideas, but alas! we understand not their speech, and what they say brings us neither instruction nor profit.

In the Wiek, close to the shore, there dwelt in olden days a beauteous Mermaid, who oftentimes appeared to mankind; indeed, my great-grand-father's cousin, who grew up in this region, saw her occasionally seated on a rock, but never dared approach her. The maiden appeared in various forms, now as a foal or a heifer, now as some other animal. Many an evening she would mix with the children and amuse herself playing with them, until some of the little boys mounted on her back; then she suddenly disappeared as though beneath the earth.

But old folk tell that in the early times the

beauteous maiden might be seen almost every summer evening, seated on a rock by the seashore, combing her long fair hair with a golden comb, whilst she sang in sweet strains that melted the hearts of her hearers. Yet she suffered not the approach of men, but vanished from before their eyes, or escaped into the sea, where she swam over the waves like a swan. Why she thus fled from men, and no longer felt her former confidence in them, we will now relate.

In the olden days, long before the kingdom of Sweden existed, there dwelt on the banks of the Wiek a well-to-do peasant with his wife and four sons. They gained their livelihood more from the sea than the land, for in their time fishing was very profitable. From his earliest years the youngest son had shown himself different in everything to his brothers; shunning all companionship, he would wander along the seashore, or far into the depths of the forest, and talk to himself, to the birds, to the winds and the waves, but when amongst men he rarely opened his mouth, and stood silent and apart as one in a dream. When, in the autumn, storms raged over the sea, and the waves after rising mountains high broke foaming on the shore, the boy could not rest in doors, but ran as though possessed, and often only half clothed, to the beach. Heedless of wind and weather, he would spring into the boat, seize the oars, and ride like a wild duck over the crests of the foaming waves far out to sea, yet he never suffered through his rashness. In the morning when the storm had died away he would be found sleeping peacefully on the seashore. If he were sent anywhere on business—for instance, in summer to tend the cattle, or some other work—he only vexed his parents by his carelessness and indifference. Instead of attending to his work, he would throw himself down to rest beneath a shady tree, heedless of the cattle, who, left to amuse themselves, trod down meadows or cornfields, and frequently strayed away, when his brothers often had to search for hours before they brought them safely home. His father had often beaten the boy severely for his carelessness, but beating and scolding were alike useless. When he grew up things were no better; no work ever prospered under his lazy hands: he damaged or broke the plough, exhausted the oxen, and, in short, did nothing right.

His father sent him to service in strange farms, hoping that perhaps among strangers the loiterer might become a good, industrious man ; but whoever tried him for one week always sent him back the next. His parents scolded him as an idler, and his brothers called him Sleepy Tönnis, although he had been baptized George. When, however, he became unbearable and no one would employ him, his father sent him as a servant on a strange ship, partly because he could not run away on the sea, partly because from childhood the boy had loved the water. Notwithstanding, after a few weeks, he had escaped from the ship, and was again on dry land. As he was ashamed to set foot in his parents' house, where he dared not hope for a friendly reception, he wandered from one place to another trying to gain his living without working. He was a fine, strong young fellow, and could talk very pleasantly if he liked, although in his father's house he had never troubled to speak much. Now he was obliged to make the best of himself, and use smooth words, for he knew how with them to ingratiate himself with the women and maidens.

One beautiful summer evening at the setting of the sun, as he walked alone upon the beach, the sweet song of the Mermaid fell on his ear, and looking up he beheld the lovely songstress seated on a rock combing her hair with her golden comb. Sleepy Tönnis thought, 'She is also a woman, and will not harm me,' and advanced towards her. The Mermaid observed the comer, but did not fly from him as she usually did when approached by man. Moreover, when he stopped, uncertain whether to approach nearer, she rose from her rock, and, advancing towards him with extended hand, said :

'I have waited for you for many days; a dream warned me of your arrival. Amongst mankind you have neither house nor home. Why be dependent on strangers because your parents will not shelter you ? I have known you from your youth up, and better than men know you, for I have been near you, unseen, and protected you when your temerity would otherwise have caused your destruction. Yes, these hands have ofttimes guided your fragile bark that it might not sink into the deep ! Come with me ; your days shall be full of joy; what your heart desires you shall possess. I will watch over you and guard you from all harm.'

Sleepy Tönnis scratched his ear and wondered what he should answer, although each word the maiden uttered penetrated his heart like a fiery dart. At length he asked shyly if her dwelling were far from there.

'We can go there with the swiftness of the wind, if only you have full confidence in me,' replied the Mermaid.

Suddenly Sleepy Tönnis remembered all he had heard folks tell of the Mermaid; his heart failed him, and he asked three days for reflection.

'I will grant your request,' said the Mermaid; 'but that you may not forget to return, I will, ere we part, put my gold ring on your finger. When we become better acquainted, this pledge may perhaps serve as a betrothal ring.'

With this she placed it on the youth's little finger, and disappeared.

Sleepy Tönnis stood still with open eyes; he would have held all that had passed as a dream had not the glittering ring on his finger proved the contrary. But with this ring a strange spirit of unrest had entered into him. He wandered all night along the shore, returning again and again to the rock on which the maiden had sat; but the rock was cold and bare. In the morning he lay down to sleep, but disquieting dreams destroyed his rest, and he awoke, longing for the evening that he might again behold the lovely Mermaid. The day waned, the wind dropped, the birds ceased their song, and hid their tired bills beneath their wings, but that evening the Mermaid came not.

THE MERMAID COMES BACK TO SLEEPY TÖNNIS.

Care and sorrow forced bitter tears from his eyes.
Why, oh why, had he rejected the proffered happiness, and begged time for thought, when a wiser
than he would have seized it eagerly! Now, remorse
and complaining were alike useless. Sorrowfully
passed the night, and the day following; bowed
down with sorrow, hunger was unfelt. Towards
sunset he seated himself on the rock, and, weeping
bitterly, moaned forth :

'If to-day she come not, I will live no longer, but
either perish with hunger here on this stone, or
plunge into the waves, and end this wretched life in
the depths of the sea!'

As he sat thus, a soft warm hand was laid on his
forehead. Looking up, he saw the Mermaid, who
said kindly :

'Seeing your bitter sorrow, I could delay no
longer.'

'Forgive, forgive me, dearest maiden,' sobbed
Sleepy Tönnis. 'Forgive me, I was a senseless fool.
The evil one alone knows what folly took possession
of me! Take me whither you will; I would gladly
give my life for you.'

The Mermaid smiled.

'I desire not your death,' she replied; 'rather
you shall live with me as my beloved consort.'

She then led the youth a few steps nearer the sea,
and bound a silken handkerchief over his eyes. The
same moment Sleepy Tönnis felt himself seized by
two strong arms, and plunged into the flood. As
the waves touched his body he lost consciousness.

When he awoke he was lying on a soft bed with

silken hangings, in a magnificent chamber whose walls of glass were curtained with crimson velvet; on a chair beside the bed lay beautiful clothes. For some time he was uncertain whether he still lived. Having after some reflection satisfied himself that he was still alive, he rose and dressed. Accidentally he coughed. Immediately two maidens entered, and, curtseying reverently, prayed their ' Noble Lord ' to say what he wished for breakfast. Whilst one laid the table the other departed to prepare the meal, and the table was soon covered with dishes of pork, sausages, black-puddings, and honey, together with beer and mead, just as though a grand wedding feast were spread. Sleepy Tönnis, who had not tasted food for many days, ate heartily, and then stretched himself on the bed to rest. When he again arose the maidens entered and begged their ' Noble Lord ' to walk in the garden whilst their gracious mistress performed her toilet. On all sides he was greeted as ' Noble Lord,' so he soon began to think himself really noble, and quite forgot his early life.

In the garden grace and beauty greeted him at every step; gold and silver apples glittered amongst the green leaves, even the pine and fir-trees were of gold, whilst gold-feathered birds hopped among the branches. Two maidens stepped forth from behind a bush; they had orders to lead their ' Noble Lord ' round the garden, and show him all its beauties. Further on they came to a lake, on whose smooth surface swam geese with gold and silver feathers. Over all glimmered the rosy light of morning, but the sun was nowhere to be seen. Trees covered with flowers exhaled a sweet perfume, whilst bees as large as gadflies flew about amongst the blossoms. Later, two maidens in beautiful garments appeared, to lead their 'Noble Lord' to the gracious lady who awaited him. ·Before he entered her presence a blue silk scarf was thrown round his shoulders. In this dress who could have recognised the Sleepy Tönnis of former days?

In a magnificent apartment formed of glass twelve beauteous maidens sat on silver stools. Behind them on a raised daïs were two golden chairs; on one sat the stately queen, the other was vacant. When Sleepy Tönnis entered the maidens rose, greeting him reverently, and did not resume their seats until bidden. The lady remained seated, bowed graciously to the youth, and then beckoned authoritatively with her finger, whereupon the two maidens led Sleepy Tönnis to their mistress. He approached timidly, not venturing to raise his eyes; the beauty and splendour almost blinded him. They showed him his place on the golden chair beside the queen, who, as soon as he was seated, said :

' Behold my beloved bridegroom, to whom I am betrothed, and whom I have chosen for my husband. You must show him every respect, and obey him as you do me. Whenever I leave the house you must make the time pass pleasantly to him, and see he wants for nothing. Heavy will be the punishment of anyone not obeying my commands.'

Sleepy Tönnis looked around bewildered, uncertain if he were awake or dreaming. Guessing his thoughts, the lady rose, took his hand, and led him from the apartment. After passing through eleven rooms, all empty, they entered a chamber which, though smaller, was far more beautiful than the others. Here the lady took off her crown, cast aside her gold-embroidered mantle, and when Sleepy Tönnis raised his eyes, no stranger, but his own beautiful Mermaid stood beside him. Oh, blessed time! His courage and hope at once revived; joyfully he exclaimed:

'Beloved Mermaid!' But the same moment the maiden's hand closed his mouth.

'If your own happiness and mine are dear to you,' said she earnestly, 'never again use that name; that was only given me in insult. I am a daughter of the Mother of the Waters. We are many sisters, but each dwells in her own place, in sea, in lake, and in river; we are but rarely seen, and then only through some lucky accident.'

She then explained that until now she had lived a virgin, but as the ordained sovereign she was obliged to support the name and dignity of a royal lady.

Sleepy Tönnis was almost beside himself with joy, and could only murmur 'Yes' and 'No.' Later, however, at dinner, when he had tasted many a dainty dish and costly wine, he regained his speech, and was able, not only to converse affably, but also to bring out many a pleasant jest.

For two days the same happy life was led, but the third evening, before retiring to rest, the Mermaid said:

'To-morrow is Thursday, and conformably with a solemn vow I must every week spend this day fasting and alone. Thursdays you cannot see me before the evening cock has crowed thrice. My maidens will care for you in the meantime, so you will not find the time long.'

The next morning the Mermaid was nowhere to be found. Sleepy Tönnis now remembered her words, that he must spend every Thursday without her. The servants exerted themselves to amuse him. They sang, played, and performed merry dances; then they set costly meats and drinks before him, and the day passed quicker than he could have believed. Supper ended, he retired to rest, and as the evening cock crowed the third time the lovely maiden was again at his side. Thus it happened every Thursday. Often had he entreated his beloved to allow him to fast with her, but in vain. Once, when he had tormented her more than usual with his prayers, the Mermaid replied, weeping:

'Take my life if you will, I give it willingly; but your wish to share my fast I cannot, I dare not grant.'

A year or more might have elapsed when doubts arose in the heart of Sleepy Tönnis which destroyed all his happiness. He feared the Mermaid had a secret lover, in whose arms she rested on the Thursdays, whilst he had to spend the time with her maidens. The chamber in which she concealed herself he knew well, but what help was that? The door was always locked, and the window thickly curtained. But the more impossible it appeared, the stronger became his desire to fathom the mystery. Although he said nothing to the Mermaid about the doubts that troubled his soul, she knew from his restless manner that things were no longer as they should be. Again and again she begged him with tears not to torture himself and her with preposterous suspicions.

' I am,' said she, ' free from all guilt towards you ; I have no secret lover, or any other sin against you on my conscience. But your groundless suspicion makes us both unhappy. Joyfully would I give my life for you, but on my fast-day I cannot have you near me. It may not be ; it would destroy for ever our love and happiness. We live together in peaceful happiness six days in the week : how can the separation of one day fall so heavily on you that you cannot endure it ?'

The six days comforted him as usual, but when the following Thursday the Mermaid did not appear, he lost his head and behaved like one half insane. His peace of mind was gone for ever ; soon he suffered no one to come near him on the Thursdays. The maidens dared only set down the meats and drinks, and then depart immediately.

This extraordinary change surprised everyone. When the Mermaid heard of it she wept bitterly ; yet she only indulged her grief when alone. Sleepy Tönnis hoped that when alone he might find some means of investigating the mysterious chamber. The more he tormented himself, the sadder grew the Mermaid, and although she still looked cheerful, her heart was no longer joyful.

Weeks passed, and things were no better and no worse. Then, one Thursday, Sleepy Tönnis found a little place at the window through which he could see into the room. What he saw made his heart turn cold. The mysterious chamber had no floor, but was like a great square tub, filled many feet high with water. In it swam his beloved Mermaid. From her head to her waist she still retained her beautiful woman's form, but from her waist downwards she had the form of a fish covered with scales, and provided with fins. With her broad fish's tail she lashed the water, splashing it high into the air. Sleepy Tönnis drew back stupefied, and went away full of trouble. What would he not have given to be able to efface that horrible sight from his mind?

That evening the cock crowed as usual, but the Mermaid came not. He watched the whole night through; the maiden did not appear. At daybreak she entered, clad in deep mourning, her face covered with a silk veil, and said in a tearful voice:

'Unhappy mortal! Your folly has brought our happy life to a close. To-day you see me for the last time, for you must now return to your former condition. Farewell!'

A sudden crash, and a noise as though the earth were rolling from beneath his feet, and Sleepy Tönnis fell senseless on the ground.

When he awoke he was lying on the sea-shore close to the rock where he had first seen the Mermaid. Instead of the handsome clothes he had worn in the Mermaid's dwelling, he wore his old suit, which, however, looked more old and ragged than from his recollection of his fall should have been the case. His happy days were ended, and no repentance, however bitter, could restore them.

Proceeding further, he came to the first farmhouse of his native village. But how strange it now appeared. Moreover, the people were all strangers to him, and nowhere did he recognise a familiar face.

They also looked curiously at him, as though he were some wonderful animal. He sought his childhood's home; here also strangers met him. Astonished, he asked for his father and brothers, but no one could give him any information. Then a feeble old man came out, leaning on a staff, and said:

'Peasant, the man you seek has slept beneath the earth these thirty years; his sons also are dead. From whence come you then, old man, to ask after these forgotten?'

The greeting 'old man' terrified Sleepy Tönnis; his limbs trembled, and, turning his back on the strangers, he hastened from the door.

At the next brook he beheld his own form in the watery mirror; the wrinkled cheeks, sunken eyes, long gray beard and gray hair, confirmed what he had heard. This yellow, withered form bore no resemblance to the youth the Mermaid had chosen as a bridegroom. The unfortunate man now first realized that what to him had seemed two years was in reality a greater part of his life; as a youth he had entered the Mermaid's dwelling, as a spectre-like old man he returned. There he had felt neither the flight of time nor decay of body. What would now become of him, a stranger amongst strangers? For many days he wandered along the shore from one farm to another, and the good folks, pitying him, gave him food. Once he met a peasant to whom he related the history of his life; the same night he disappeared. A few days later his dead body was washed ashore.

From that time the ways of the Mermaid towards men have entirely altered; to children she sometimes appears, but generally in other forms; men, however, she never suffers to approach her, but shuns them like fire.

FORTUNE'S EGG.

NCE upon a time a poor man and his wife dwelt in a large forest. Heaven had given them eight children, most of whom were already earning their bread amongst strangers, therefore it did not give the parents much pleasure when in their old age a ninth little son was born to them. Still, Heaven had sent him, so they were obliged to put up with him, and have him baptized according to Christian custom. But no one would stand godfather to the infant, for each said :

'When the parents die the child will fall a burden on me.'

Then the father thought, ' I will carry the child to the church on Sunday, and say that nowhere can I find godparents for him ; then the priest may do as he will ; he may baptize him or not—no sin will rest on my soul.'

As he set out on Sunday he saw a beggar seated by the roadside, who asked for alms. The father said :

' I have nothing to give you, little brother ; the few copecks I have in my pocket I must pay for the

child's baptism. Will you, however, do me a kind-
ness? Come and stand godfather to my child;
afterwards we will go home and share whatever my
wife has prepared for the christening breakfast.'

The beggar, who had never before been asked to
stand godfather, joyfully granted the father's request,
and went with him to the church. Just as they
arrived a beautiful coach with four horses drove up,
and a young and stately lady alighted. The poor
man thought, ' I will try my luck for the last time,'
and stepping up to the lady said, bowing reverently,
' Gracious lady, or maiden, whichever you may be,
would it be troubling you too much to stand godmother to my child ?' The lady consented.

When, after the sermon, the child was brought to
the font the priest and congregation marvelled
greatly that a poor beggar and a proud, high-born
lady should together stand sponsors to the babe.
The child received the name of Pärtel. The rich
godmother paid the christening fee and gave a
christening present of three roubles, at which the
father was much pleased. The beggar returned with
him to the breakfast. Before leaving in the evening
he took a small box from his pocket, carefully
wrapped in rags, gave it to the child's mother, and
said :

' My christening present is insignificant, but do
not despise it on that account ; perhaps when he
grows up your son may gain some happiness through
it. I had a clever aunt who understood all kinds of
magic arts ; before her death she gave me the bird's
egg in this little box, saying, " If ever you meet with

something quite unexpected, something you could never have anticipated, renounce this egg, for it will then bring great happiness to the person on whom it is bestowed. But guard it carefully that it does not break, for fortune's shell is brittle." Now, although I have lived nearly sixty years, I have never met anything unexpected until to-day, when I was asked to be a godfather, and immediately I thought, You must give the egg to the child as a christening present.'

Little Pärtel throve wonderfully, and grew up a joy to his parents, but when he was ten years old he was sent into another village as shepherd boy to a well-to-do farmer. Everyone in the house was well satisfied with the boy, for he was a pious, quiet child, and never neglected his employer's business. On taking leave of him, his mother put his christening present in his pocket, bidding him guard it carefully, a command that Pärtel strictly obeyed. In the midst of the pasture stood an old linden-tree, beneath which lay a large stone; this place the boy loved so, that in summer not a day passed without his having sat on this stone. Here also he usually ate the bread that was given him every morning, quenching his thirst at the little brook close by. For the other shepherd boys, who were full of mischief, Pärtel had no liking. Wonderful it was that nowhere was the grass so beautiful as between the rock and the brook, and although the flocks grazed there every day, by the following morning the grass had more the appearance of a lovely meadow than of a pasture.

Sometimes when the days were sultry, Pärtel fell asleep on the stone. Then beautiful dreams visited him, and on awakening sweet songs and music still sounded in his ears, so that he dreamed on with open eyes. The old stone was to him as a dear friend from whom he daily parted with a heavy heart, and to whom he eagerly returned the next morning. When young Pärtel was fifteen years old the farmer took him as a labourer, without, however, giving him harder work than he was able to perform. On Sunday evenings in summer, when the other lads jested with the maidens, Pärtel pensively sought his linden-tree, beneath which he not unfrequently passed half the night. As he sat thus one evening playing on the Jew's-harp, a milk-white snake crept from beneath the stone, raised its head as though wishing to listen, and gazed at Pärtel with its bright eyes that glittered like fiery sparks. This recurred frequently, and now whenever Pärtel had any spare time he always hastened to his stone to see the beautiful white snake, who soon grew so used to him that it would wind itself round his knees.

By this time Pärtel had grown to man's estate; his parents were dead, and all his brothers and sisters lived far away, so that they rarely heard from each other. But the white snake was dearer to him than brother or sister; he thought of it by day and dreamed of it by night. For this reason the winter, when the ground was frozen and snow covered the land, seemed to him a very weary time. But when the spring sunbeams had melted the snow, Pärtel hastened to the stone beneath the linden-tree, although as yet no leaves were to be seen on the branches. Oh, the joy! As soon as he began to breathe forth his longings in the notes of the Jew's-harp, the white snake crept from beneath the stone and played about his feet, but to-day it seemed to him as though the snake shed tears, and this made his heart sad. Now no evening passed without his visiting the stone, and the snake, becoming ever more confident, soon allowed itself to be stroked; but if Pärtel wished to hold it, it slipped through his fingers and crept beneath the stone.

On Midsummer Eve all the villagers, both young and old, went to the St. John's fire, and Pärtel dared not stay behind, although his heart drew him another way. But in the midst of the gaiety, whilst the others sang, danced, and played merry games, he crept back to the old linden-tree, for here alone his heart knew rest. As he approached, a small, bright fire gleamed towards him from the stone, which greatly astonished him, for, as far as he knew, all had gone to the merry-making. When he reached the stone the fire had disappeared. He seated himself and began as usual to play his Jew's-harp. The same moment the fire again shone forth; it was nothing less than the sparkling eyes of the beautiful white snake. It crept to his feet, let him stroke it, and gazed at him searchingly, as though wishing to speak. Midnight was not far distant when the snake crept back to its nest beneath the stone; and although Pärtel continued his playing it did not return. At length, taking the instrument from his mouth, he placed it in his pocket and prepared to

return home ; then the leaves of the old linden-tree
began to rustle so strangely in the breath of the
night wind, that it fell on his ear like the tones of a
human voice, repeating again and again the words :

> ' Fortune's egg has a tender shell,
> And a kernel hard is sorrow.
> When happiness comes, grasp it well,
> And nothing fear for the morrow.'

Then such sad deep longing fell on him that his
heart threatened to break, yet he knew not for what
he longed.   Bitter tears flowed down his cheeks, and
he moaned :

' Of what use is Fortune's egg to me, the unfortunate?   No happiness has ever visited me!   From
earliest childhood I have been unlike other folks·
They do not understand me, nor do I understand
them.   What gives them pleasure causes me pain ;
what would make me happy I know not myself ; how
then can others know?   Riches and poverty stood
together as my sponsors, therefore nothing can come
right for me.'

As he spoke all around grew bright as though both
linden-tree and stone were bathed in sunlight.   So
bright was it that for a time Pärtel was unable to
open his eyes.   When, however, he had grown
accustomed to the light, he saw standing beside the
stone a lovely female form clad in snow-white
garments, and looking like an angel just descended
from heaven.   The maiden spoke, and the tone of
her voice sounded to him sweeter than the song of
the nightingale.

'Dear youth,' said she, 'fear not, but grant the prayer of an unfortunate maiden. I live in a miserable prison, and, should you not take pity on me, I have no hope of deliverance. Oh, dearest youth, do not refuse my prayer. I am the daughter of an Eastern King. I have countless riches in gold and treasures, but this helps me not, for a magic spell compels me to dwell beneath this stone in the form of a snake, and here I have already passed many hundred years without growing old. Although I have never harmed a single creature, all fly from my form the moment I appear. You alone have not shunned my approach; thus I dared to play around your feet, your hand also has often stroked me tenderly. Then there arose within me the hope that you would be my deliverer. Your heart is white and pure as that of a child to whom lying and deceit are as yet unknown. Besides this you possess all that is necessary for my deliverance—a high-born lady and a beggar stood together as your sponsors, and the egg of fortune was your christening present. On Midsummer's Eve once in every five and twenty years I am permitted to wander over the earth for one hour in human form; if then a youth of pure heart, and possessing this rare gift, comes by and grants my prayer, I can be freed from my lifelong imprisonment. Save, oh save me from endless captivity, I entreat you in the name of all the angels in heaven !'

Thus saying, she fell at his feet, embraced his knees and wept bitterly.

Pärtel's heart melted at the sight of her grief; he

SHE FELL AT HIS FEET AND WEPT BITTERLY.

entreated the maiden to rise, and tell him how he could save her.

'I would without hesitation go through fire and water,' said he, 'if thereby your deliverance became possible, and had I ten lives I would sacrifice them willingly to save you! A longing I cannot understand leaves me no peace, but what I long for I know not!'

The maiden replied :

'Come hither to-morrow at sunset, and if I then approach you in the form of a snake, wind myself round your waist like a girdle and kiss you thrice, shrink not, and be not afraid, otherwise I must continue to sigh beneath this spell for who knows how many hundred years.'

With these words she disappeared, and again the leaves of the old linden-tree sighed forth :

> ' Fortune's egg has a tender shell,
> And a kernel hard is sorrow.
> When happiness comes, grasp it well,
> And nothing fear for the morrow.'

Pärtel hastened home and lay down to sleep, but strange dreams, at times pleasant, at times hateful, chased rest from his pillow. At length he awoke with a loud cry from a dream that the white snake had wound itself round his body and bitten him. It is true that on awakening he paid no further heed to the fearful dream, and was still resolved to set the Princess free, even though he should perish in the attempt ; yet, nevertheless, his heart grew heavier the nearer the sun approached the horizon.

At the appointed hour he stood beside the stone, and sighing, looked towards heaven, entreating courage and strength, that he might not tremble with weakness when the snake wound itself round his body and kissed him. Suddenly, remembering his christening present, he took the box from his pocket, unwrapped it, and took the little egg, that was no larger than the egg of a hedge-sparrow, between his fingers.

The same moment the snow-white snake had crept from beneath the stone, wound itself round his body, and was just raising its head to kiss him, when—the youth knew not how it happened—he placed the egg in the snake's mouth. Then he stood without trembling, though with freezing heart, while the snake kissed him thrice. Immediately there followed a noise and a flash as though lightning had struck the stone, whilst loud thunder made the earth tremble so that Pärtel fell to the ground as dead, and no longer knew what happened to him, or around him.

But in that dread moment the bands of the enchantment were broken, and the royal maiden was freed from her long imprisonment. On awakening from his swoon, Pärtel found himself lying on soft silk cushions, in a magnificent chamber formed of glass of a heavenly blue colour. Beside him knelt the Princess, who, as soon as he opened his eyes, exclaimed:

'Thanks be to Heaven, who has heard my prayer! and a thousand, thousand thanks to you, dear youth, for setting me free! Take as your reward my kingdom, this magnificent royal castle, with all its treasures, and, if you will, me as your wife. From henceforth you shall live in happiness, as becomes the Lord of Fortune's Egg. Until to-day your lot was that of your godfather, now a better fortune awaits you, one that would have been pleasing to your godmother.'

None can describe Pärtel's joy and happiness ; the restless longing that had driven him again and again to the old linden-tree was now stilled. Separated from the world, he lived with his wife in the lap of fortune until his end.

In the village, and in the farm where he had served, Pärtel's disappearance caused great anxiety, and everyone went out to search for him. Their first journey was to the linden-tree that the youth used to visit so constantly, and whither he had been seen going the previous evening. Great was their astonishment when they found neither Pärtel, nor the linden-tree, nor even the stone ; moreover, the little brook was dried up, and no human eye has ever again beheld them.

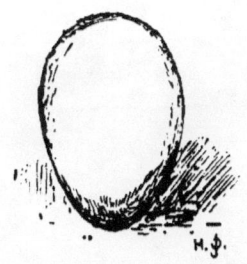

THE NORTHLAND DRAGON.

THE

NORTHLAND DRAGON.

N olden times, according to the traditions of our forefathers, there lived a horrible monster that had come from Northland. He had already denuded large districts of both man and beast, and had no one found a remedy he would gradually have destroyed every living thing from off the face of the earth.

He had the body of an ox, a tail like a snake's, ten fathoms long, and legs like a frog; moreover, he moved like a frog, and travelled half a mile at each spring. Fortunately for mankind, after once settling down in a place he remained there many years, and did not move on further until he had devastated the surrounding regions. His body was covered with many coats of scales, each stronger than stone or iron, so nothing could harm him. His great eyes glittered day and night like the brightest tapers, and anyone having the misfortune to glance at their splendour was as one bewitched, and of his own free will rushed into the monster's jaws. The kings of the neighbouring countries promised enormous rewards to anyone who should destroy the horrible monster; many had tried, but all their efforts were vain. Once a forest in which the monster dwelt was ·set on fire; the forest was burnt down, but without the fire doing the least harm to the animal it was intended to destroy. Tradition said no one could overcome the monster without the aid of King Solomon's signet-ring, on which was a secret writing telling how the monster might be destroyed. Only none knew where the ring was now concealed, and they knew just as little where to find a magician skilful enough to interpret the writing.

At length a young man, whose heart and head were in the right place, resolved to seek this ring. He took the way that led towards the East, and, after several years of travel, met a celebrated Eastern magician, and asked his advice.

The magician replied:

'The infinitesimal wisdom of man cannot avail you here. God's birds will be your best guides if you will learn their language. I can help you to do this if you remain with me a few days.'

The youth joyfully accepted the kindly invitation, and said:

'I cannot recompense you at present, but, should my enterprise end happily, I will richly repay your trouble.'

From nine different kinds of roots, gathered secretly by moonlight, the magician made a strong drink, and of this he gave the young man nine spoonfuls daily for three days, with the result that at

the end of that time the bird language was quite in-
telligible to him. On his leaving, the magician said :
' Should you have the good fortune to discover King
Solomon's ring, and obtain possession of it, return
at once to me, that I may decipher the writing, for,
beside me, no one now lives who understands it.'

When he set forth, the youth discovered with
surprise he was no longer alone, but had companionship wherever he turned, for he understood the
language of birds, and through this much became
clear that human wisdom had been unable to teach
him. Some time, however, elapsed ere he heard
anything of the ring. One evening, wearied with
travel, he sat down to rest beneath a tree in the
forest. On a high branch overhead, two birds with
gay plumage were conversing. The first bird said :

' I know the visionary beneath the tree. He has
wandered about for years without success. He seeks
the long-lost ring of King Solomon.'

The other made answer :

' He must seek aid from the Maid of the Infernal
Regions. She alone can put him on the right track·
If she has not the ring herself, she certainly knows
who has it.'

The first bird replied :

' That is true. But how to find the Maid of the
Infernal Regions ? She has no permanent abode,
but dwells here to-day, there to-morrow. He might
as well strive to chain the wind.'

To this the second bird :

' I know not her present abode, but three days
hence she will come, as she does every month on the

night of the full moon, to bathe her face at the spring, that the beauty of youth may never fade from her cheek, nor the wrinkles of age gather on her brow.'

The first said :

'The spring is not far distant : shall we go and watch her doings ?'

'With all my heart,' replied the other.

The youth immediately determined to follow the birds. He was too tired to remain awake the whole night, yet fear of oversleeping himself did not suffer him to rest quietly, and he often started up, think-ing the birds had set forth without him. Great, therefore, was his rejoicing when, on looking up into the branches at sunrise, he saw the bright-coloured companions still sitting with their heads tucked under their feathers. He breakfasted, and then awaited the birds' departure. This morning, however, they seemed to have no desire for travel, but fluttered from one bough to another, either for amuse-ment or in search of food, and at eve retired to rest in the old place. The same occurred the following day. The third morning, at daybreak, one bird said :

'To-day we must fly to the spring.'

However, they lingered until mid-day, and then flew away towards the south. The youth's heart beat fast through fear he should lose sight of his guides. But, after flying a short distance, they again settled on the branch of a tree. The youth ran swiftly after them. After resting thrice, the birds reached a small plain, at the edge of which they once more settled on the branch of a tall tree. Great was the youth's joy when, on reaching the spot, he beheld a spring in the centre of the plain. He therefore sat down to rest beneath the tree on whose branches the birds had perched ; then he listened attentively, that he might not miss one word of their conversation.

'The sun has not yet set,' said one bird. 'We have some time to wait ere the moon rises and the maiden comes to the spring. Do you think she will notice the youth beneath the tree ?'

His companion replied :

'Her eyes never fail to see a young man. Will the youth be wise enough not to be entangled by her wiles ?'

To which the first made answer :

'We shall see how they get on together.'

The evening was past, and the full moon had risen high above the forest, when the youth heard a slight noise, and a maiden stepped from out the forest and moved with light, swift step to the spring. Never had the youth beheld a lovelier maiden. He could not turn away his eyes from her.

Without noticing him, the maiden approached the spring, raised her eyes to the moon, then, falling on her knees, dipped her face nine times in the water. After each time she looked towards the moon, crying:

'Radiant and bright as thou now art, so may my beauty bloom everlastingly.'

Then she walked nine times round the spring, singing each time the following refrain :

'May my maiden beauty ne'er decay,
Nor the bloom on my cheek grow pale.
Though the moon herself should pass away,
May my happiness never fail !'

Then she dried her face with her long hair, and was just turning away when her eyes fell on the youth seated beneath the tree. Immediately she turned her steps thither. The youth rose and awaited her arrival.

The beauteous maid approached and said :

'By rights a heavy punishment should fall on you for watching the Maid of the Infernal Regions and her secret doings in the moonlight ; but, as you are a stranger, and arrived here accidentally, I will forgive you. Yet you must tell me truly whence you come, and how you journeyed hither, where until now no mortal man has ever set foot.'

The youth replied :

'Forgive me, dearest maiden, if unknowingly I have offended you. Arriving hither after long travel, I resolved to pass the night beneath these trees.'

The maid replied :

'Come, pass the night with us. It is better to rest on cushions than on soft cool moss.'

The youth remained a moment undecided ; he knew not whether to accept or to reject the kindly invitation. Then one of the birds said :

'He were a fool not to be delighted with the invitation.'

The maiden, who was unacquainted with the bird language, continued :

'Fear nothing, my friend ; I have no evil intention towards you.'

The birds overhead said :

'Go with her ; but beware of giving blood, for with blood you sell your soul.'

The youth went. Close to the spring was a beautiful garden, in which stood a magnificent residence, that glittered in the moonlight as though formed of gold and silver. In its spacious halls many hundred candles in golden candlesticks shed over all a light like that of day. In a magnificent apartment was a table spread with costly meats; by it stood two chairs, one of silver, the other of gold. The maiden seated herself on the golden chair, and bade the youth take the other. Maidens in white raiment handed the dishes and bore them away, but no word was spoken. After the repast, when the youth was alone with the regal maiden, a pleasant conversation was carried on, until a waiting-maid clad in red came to summon them to rest.

The maiden then showed the youth an apartment where a silken bed with down pillows was prepared. Then she departed. Of what occurred during that night he could never form any decided opinion, but remained uncertain whether he had dreamed or whether he had really heard voices calling to him in tones that made his heart tremble:

'Give no blood! Give no blood!'

The next morning the maiden asked if he would not like to remain with her, and, when he did not immediately answer, added:

'I am, as you see, young and beautiful. I own no one's sway, and can do whatever pleases me. Until now it never entered my mind to marry, but the moment I saw you other thoughts arose within me. Should our thoughts agree, we could marry. Lands and goods I possess in abundance. I live

'THIS IS MY DEAREST TREASURE,' SHE SAID.

in queenly splendour. Whatever you desire I can provide.'

These tender words threatened to confuse the youth's heart; but fortunately he remembered the birds had called her the Maid of the Infernal Regions, and had warned him against giving his blood. Therefore he replied:

'Dearest maiden, be not angry that I cannot at once reply to your kind and gracious proposal, and grant me, I pray you, a few days for reflection.'

'Wherefore not?' replied the maid. 'So far as I am concerned you may think for a few weeks.'

She then led the youth through her beautiful mansion and showed him all its rich treasures. These were, however, obtained through magic, for by the aid of King Solomon's ring the maiden could every day raise up a like dwelling and all its riches. But they had no duration; they were blown together by the winds, and by the winds they were dispersed, leaving no trace behind. As the youth did not know this, he took the delusion for reality. One day she led him into a secret chamber, where, on a silver table, lay a small gold box. She showed it him, saying:

'Here lies my dearest treasure—a costly gold ring; its like cannot be found in the whole world. If you marry me, I will give it you as dowry, and it will make you the happiest of men. But that our love may be eternal, you must in return give me three drops of blood from the little finger of your left hand.'

When the youth heard these words a cold shiver

6

thrilled his frame, for he remembered that his blood was required to purchase his soul. Still, he was wise enough not to show his repugnance ; indeed, he asked, as though accidentally, what properties this ring possessed that made it so valuable. The maiden replied :

'Up to the present no living person has been able to fathom its power, for none can fully decipher its secret signs. But with only a half knowledge I perform wonders which I can accomplish in no other way. I place this ring on the little finger of my left hand, then like a bird I can fly whither I will. I place it on the ring finger, I am invisible to all ; I see, but others see me not. I place the ring on my left middle finger, then neither sharp instrument, nor fire, nor water, can harm me. I put it on the forefinger, immediately I can secure all things I desire. Place the ring on the left thumb, and the hand becomes so strong it can break rocks and walls. Besides, this ring has many secret signs, which, as I have said, no one has yet been able to decipher. In olden times it belonged to King Solomon, the wisest of all kings. But no one has ever been able to discover if the ring was formed by heavenly might, or by human hands. It is believed that an angel gave it to the wise king.'

Hearing this, the youth's first thought was to gain possession of the ring. He therefore pretended not to believe what he heard, hoping this would move the maiden to take the ring from its box, when he might perchance have an opportunity to possess himself of the treasure. He did not venture to ask her to show it to him. He flattered and caressed her tenderly, but all the time his heart was thinking only of how to obtain possession of the ring.

The maiden took a key from her bosom, and was about to unlock the little box, when she hesitated a few moments, then saying, ' We have not time now,' replaced the key.

A few days later the conversation again turned on the magic ring, and the youth said :

' In my opinion, what you have told me about your ring is absolutely impossible.'

The maiden smiled, and, opening the casket, took out the ring. Then, for sport, she placed the sparkling jewel on the middle finger of her left hand, telling the youth to take a knife and stab her where he would, for he could not hurt her. The youth objected ; but when she persisted, he joined in the sport. He tried in all ways to strike the maiden, at first playfully, later in earnest ; but it was as though an invisible wall of ice stood between them, which the knife could not penetrate. Then she placed the ring on her third finger ; immediately she had disappeared, but a few moments later stood laughing before him, holding the ring between her fingers.

' Let me see,' pleaded the youth, ' if I can do such wonderful things.'

Suspecting no deception, she gave him the ring. As if he had not yet a thorough knowledge of the ring, the youth asked :

' On which finger must I place the ring so that no sharp instrument can harm me ?'

The maiden replied :

' On the left middle finger.'

She then took a knife, and tried to stab him ; but in vain. He next asked how to split stones and rocks. She led him into the courtyard, where lay an enormous rock.

' Now,' said she, 'place this ring on your left thumb, and strike the stone with your fist.'

He did as directed, and behold ! the stone was shattered into a thousand fragments. Then the youth reflected :

' Who knows not how to seize fortune by the horns is but a poor fool ; who flies away never returns.'

While still jesting, he slipped the ring on his ring finger. The maiden cried :

' Now you are invisible until you draw off the ring.' But this was not the youth's intention. Hastening away a few paces, he placed the ring on the little finger of his left hand, and soared as a bird into the air. When the maiden saw him fly away she thought he was still in sport, and called, ' Come back, come back, my friend. You see, all I told you is true.'

But the youth heeded not. Then, perceiving how she had been deceived, the maiden broke into bitter lamentations over her misfortune.

The youth paused not in his flight until he reached the magician's dwelling. The old man was overjoyed at his success, and immediately began to interpret the secret writing ; but seven weeks elapsed ere his task was concluded. Then he instructed the youth how to kill the Northland Dragon.

'First an iron horse must be made, with wheels under each foot, that it can be pushed backwards and forwards. You must mount this horse, armed with a spear two fathoms long, which you can only use by placing the ring on your left thumb. The centre of the spear must be the thickness of a large birch-tree. It must be sharpened at both ends, and in the centre you must fasten two iron chains ten fathoms long, and strong enough to secure the terrible monster. Directly the monster has bitten the spear so fast that it pierces his jawbone, spring swiftly from the horse, and fasten the ends of the chains into the earth. After three or four days the Dragon's strength will be so exhausted that you can approach him without fear; then place King Solomon's ring on your left thumb, and strike the monster dead. All being successfully accomplished, take care not to lose the ring, and be sure the jewel is not taken from you through treachery.'

The youth thanked the old man, and promised to reward him later, but the magician replied :

'I have gained so much knowledge of magic through deciphering the secrets on the ring that I require nothing further.'

Then they parted, and the youth hastened home, which, now he could fly, was no longer difficult.

Shortly after his return he heard that the horrible Northland Dragon was in the neighbourhood, and so close that he could come over the border every day. Then the King issued a proclamation that whoever killed this monster should receive not only a large portion of his kingdom, but also his daughter in marriage. Presenting himself before the King, the youth declared he could destroy the Dragon if the King would provide everything necessary thereto. The King agreeing, the most skilful workmen were immediately summoned. First the iron horse was made, then the great spear was cut, and lastly, the heavy iron chains were formed with rings two ells thick. But when finished the horse was so heavy that one hundred men could not move it. The youth was therefore obliged to take it away alone, with the aid of the magic ring.

By this time the Dragon was so close that two springs brought him over the border. The youth now considered how best to prepare to meet the monster. Being obliged to push the horse from behind, he could not mount it as the magician had directed. But a raven croaked:

'Mount the horse, and push the spear against the ground as though pushing a boat from the shore.'

The youth obeyed, and now travelled quite easily. The monster opened his enormous jaws to devour his expected prey. The youth trembled, and his heart turned cold, yet he never swerved from his purpose, but thrust the spear into the monster's mouth with such force that it went right through his jaws. Then he sprang like lightning from his horse, and not a moment too soon, for the terrible animal closed his jaws immediately, and a horrible roar, that was heard miles distant, told that the Northland Dragon had bitten the spear. Looking round, the youth saw that one point of the spear projected from the monster's upper jaw, whilst the other stuck fast in the ground. The Dragon had shattered the iron horse with his teeth. The youth now fastened the chains to the ground with strong iron pegs.

The animal's death struggles lasted three days and three nights; he roared, and struck the ground so violently with his tail that the earth shook for ten miles round. When his tail could no longer move, the youth, with the aid of the ring, raised a stone that twenty men would have been unable to move, and struck the animal on the head until all signs of life had departed.

Great were the rejoicings over the death of the terrible enemy. The Princess willingly married the victor, and a few days later a magnificent wedding was celebrated, which lasted four weeks, and at which all the neighbouring kings assembled to thank the man who had delivered the world from its worst enemy. But whilst celebrating the wedding, everyone forgot that the corpse of the Dragon remained unburied, and, as a natural consequence, the smell became terrible, and a pestilence broke out that swept away many hundreds. The youth therefore determined again to seek the magician's aid. With the help of the ring he changed himself into a bird, and flew swiftly towards the East.

But the proverb says, 'Goods unrighteously acquired never prosper,' and 'Lightly come, lightly go.' This the youth should have remembered. The Maid of the Infernal Regions ceased not day or night from trying to discover her lost treasure. When, through her magic art, she learnt that the youth was journeying in the form of a bird to the magician's dwelling, she changed herself into an eagle, and circled about in the air until her prey came in sight. She recognised him immediately by the ring that encircled his throat. Down swooped the eagle on the unsuspecting bird, and seizing him with her talons, tore the ring from his throat with her beak. The eagle then descended to earth with her prey, and the two stood face to face in human form.

'Now you are in my power, wretch!' cried the Maid of the Infernal Regions. 'I took you as my beloved; treachery and theft were my reward! You stole my costly jewel, and thought as prince to lead a happy life. Now the page is turned, now you shall receive the punishment your treachery deserves.'

'Forgive, forgive,' entreated the unlucky youth. 'I sinned grievously against you, but I repent with my whole heart.'

'Your prayers and repentance come too late,' replied the maiden; 'nothing now can help you. Through you I have been deceived and brought to shame. Your sin against me was twofold: first, you despised my love; secondly, you stole my ring; now you must suffer the punishment.'

Saying this, she placed the ring on her left thumb, took the youth under her arm like a bundle of tow, and carried him away to a rocky cavern, where chains hung from every wall. These she fastened round his hands and feet so that he could not escape. Then she said scornfully :

' Here you shall remain imprisoned until your death. Each day sufficient food will be brought to prevent your dying of hunger, but you need never hope for deliverance !' With that she left him.

The King and his daughter grew very anxious when week after week passed and nothing was heard of the youth. The Princess constantly dreamed that her husband was suffering grievous torments, and she at length asked her father to summon magicians from all parts of the world in order to gain tidings of the lost one. But the magicians could only discover that he still lived, and was enduring grievous torments ; none could tell where he dwelt, nor how he could be delivered. At length a celebrated magician from Finland stood before the King, and said that the youth was detained a prisoner in the Eastern land by the power of a mighty spirit. The King immediately sent messengers into every known kingdom to seek his beloved son-in-law. By good fortune they came to the dwelling of the old magician who had deciphered the writing on King Solomon's ring. He soon found out about the unfortunate youth, and said :

' The man you seek is held prisoner by magic art, and without my aid you cannot free him. I must go with you.'

They set forth, and, guided by the birds, soon reached the rocky cavern where the youth had already been imprisoned seven years. He recognised the magician immediately, but the magician did not recognise him, so pale and emaciated he had become. Through his magic the magician loosened the chains, and freed the unhappy prisoner ; then he took him home and tended him until he was strong enough to travel. He arrived home the day the old King died, and was at once proclaimed King. Thus after years of sorrow came years of joy, which lasted until his death, but he never again beheld the wonderful ring, nor has it since then ever been seen by human eye.

TONTLA FOREST.

TONTLA·FOREST

IN Allentacken, a district to the north of the Peipus Lake, there stood in olden times a beautiful forest called Tontla Forest, which no man dared enter. Having gone near accidentally, some bold folk had stayed to spy, and told how they had seen a ruined house amongst the trees, and round about it human beings, with whom the grass was alive, as with a swarm of ants. These creatures were sooty and ragged like gipsies, and there was amongst them an especially large number of old women and half-naked children. One dark night also a peasant returning from a feast had strayed somewhat deeper into Tontla Forest, and he had seen very strange things. Around a bright fire were numbers of women and children, some seated on the ground, others dancing on the grass. One old woman held in her hand a large iron ladle, with which from time to time she scattered the glowing embers over the grass. At this, with loud shrieks, all the children sprang into the air, whence, after fluttering like night owls amidst the

rising smoke, they descended again to earth. Then
from out the forest stepped a little old man with a
long beard, carrying on his back a sack longer than
himself! Women and children rushed tumultuously
towards him, and strove to tear the sack from his
back, but the old man shook them off. At the same
time a large black cat, with glowing, fiery eyes, that
had been sitting on the threshold, sprang on the old
man's sack, and then disappeared within the hut.
But as by this time the peasant's head began to
burn, and the objects danced before his eyes, his
story remained uncertain, and no one could ever
rightly gather what was true and what was false.

Strange it is, that although from generation to
generation weird tales were circulated concerning
Tontla Forest, none ever knew exactly what to
believe. More than once the Swedish King had
issued orders for this fearful forest to be felled, but
no one ever dared obey the command. One bold
man struck his axe into a few of the trees, but
immediately blood flowed forth, and cries of sorrow
resounded on all sides, as from human beings in
torment. The horrified woodcutter fled from the
place shaking and trembling; since then no command, however stringent, no reward, however great,
could again induce a woodcutter to enter the Forest
of Tontla. It also seemed very wonderful that there
was neither a path leading out of the forest, nor a
path leading in, and that throughout the whole year
no smoke was seen to rise, which would surely have
marked the existence of human habitations. Large
the forest was not, and all around stretched miles of

open country, so that one had a full view of it on every side. If, indeed, human beings ever dwelt there, they must have gone in and out by some subterranean passage, unless, like the witches, they rode through the air by night when all around were wrapt in slumber. According to the stories told, the latter method is the more probable. Perhaps we may gain further information concerning these marvellous beings if we guide the carriage of this narrative a little further and bring it out in the next village.

A few miles from Tontla Forest was a large village. In it dwelt a peasant, a widower, who, having had the misfortune to lose his first wife, had married again a young woman, and, as often happens, had brought a veritable firebrand into his house, so that there was no end to the scolding and wrangling. The peasant's daughter by his first wife, little seven-year-old Elspeth, was a clever, thoughtful little maiden, and the wicked stepmother made this poor child's life a perfect misery to her; she thumped and cuffed her from morning till night, gave her worse food than the dogs, and, as the woman ruled the house, the child could obtain no help from her father. For more than two years Elspeth bore this hard life, and many and bitter were the tears she shed. On Sunday she went with the other village children to gather strawberries. Rambling about after the manner of children, they came without noticing it to the edge of Tontla Forest, where beautiful strawberries grew so thickly that the grass was quite red with them. Suddenly one of the older boys, recognising the place, cried :

' Fly, fly ! we are in Tontla Forest !'

These words were more terrible than even thunder and lightning; the children immediately took to flight as though the Tontla demons were already close to their heels. Elspeth, who had gone somewhat further into the forest than the others, and had found some very beautiful berries beneath the trees, heard the boy's cry, but could not make up her mind to part from the patch of fruit. Moreover, she thought, ' The inhabitants of Tontla cannot be worse than my stepmother at home.' Presently a little black dog with a silver bell round his neck came barking towards her. At this sound a pretty little maiden in a beautiful silk dress hastened forward, ordering the dog to be quiet, and then, turning to Elspeth, said :

' I am so glad you did not run away with the other children. Stay here and be my companion, then we will play beautiful games, and go every day to gather berries; my mother I am sure will consent if I ask her. Come, let us go to her at once.'

So saying, the pretty little stranger seized Elspeth by the hand, and led her further into the forest. The little black dog now barked with pleasure, and, jumping up at Elspeth, licked her hand as though she were an old acquaintance.

Ah, what wonders now arose before Elspeth's astonished eyes ! She imagined herself in heaven. Before her lay a garden filled with cherry-trees and strawberry plants. On the branches of the trees sat birds with plumage gayer than the most brilliant butterfly, whilst some were covered with gold and

silver feathers. And the birds were not shy, but
let the children take them in their hands at their
pleasure. In the centre of the garden stood a
house built entirely of glass and precious stones,
so that the walls and roof glittered like the sun.
On a bench before the door was a lady in beautiful
garments, who, as they approached, said :

'What guest do you bring here, my child ?'

The little one replied :

'I found her alone in the forest, and brought her
home to be my companion. You will allow her to
remain, will you not, dearest mother ?'

The lady smiled, but made no reply, only glanced
keenly at Elspeth. Then bidding her step nearer,
she stroked her cheeks, asked kindly where her home
was, if her parents still lived, and whether she
would like to remain with them. For answer,
Elspeth kissed the lady's hand, and falling at her
feet, embraced her knees, whilst amidst a torrent of
tears she said :

'My mother has long rested beneath the grass.
My father, it is true, still lives, but what help is that
to me? My stepmother hates me, and beats me
mercilessly every day. Nothing I do pleases her.
I entreat you, gracious lady dressed in gold, let me
remain with you. Set me to tend the flocks, or give
me any other work. I will do anything, and obey you
in all things, only do not send me back to my cruel
stepmother ! She will beat me until I am half dead,
because I did not return with the other children.'

The lady smiled and said :

'We will see what can be done.'

7

Then rising from her seat she went into the house. But her daughter said :

' Be comforted ; my mother is kind. I am sure by her look that she will grant our request when she has considered the matter a little more closely.'

Then bidding Elspeth wait, she ran after her mother. And trembling between hope and fear, Elspeth awaited the daughter's return.

The child soon returned carrying a little box, and said :

' My mother wishes us to play together to-day while she considers further about you. I hope you will stay ; I should not like to part with you. Have you ever seen the sea ?'

' The sea ?' said Elspeth opening her eyes wide in astonishment, ' What is the sea ?　I have never even heard of it.'

' You shall see it, and at once too,' replied the little lady, taking the cover off her box.

In it lay a leaf of alchemilla, a mussel-shell, and two fish-bones. On the leaf glistened two dewdrops ; these the child shook on to the grass, and whatever had been there formerly, disappeared, as though the earth had swallowed them, and so far as the eye could see only water was visible. Beneath their feet, however, one small spot of dry, hard land remained. The little maiden placed the mussel-shell on the water and took the fish bones in her hands. The mussel-shell then became a pretty boat in which a dozen children or even more could easily have found room ; the fish-bones changed to oars. The children seated themselves in the boat, Elspeth

timidly, the other child laughing. Gradually other
boats approached filled with people who sang and
were merry.

' We must answer their song,' said the little maid,
and began to sing sweetly.

Elspeth did not understand singing. She could
not understand what was sung, but one word,
' Kiisike,' was repeated again and again. On her
asking its meaning, the child replied :

' That is my name.'

After they had rowed about for some time, a voice
called ' Children, come home ; it is evening.' Kiisike
took the leaf out of the box and dipped it in the
water, taking care that a few drops remained hang-
ing to it; immediately they were in the centre of
the garden, close to the beautiful house ; the water
had disappeared, and all was dry and firm as here-
tofore. The mussel-shell, fish-bones, and leaf were
replaced in the box, and the children went indoors.

Round a large dining-table in a spacious apartment were seated four-and-twenty ladies, dressed as
for a wedding. At the head of the table Kiisike's
mother sat on a golden chair.

Elspeth knew not whither to turn her eyes so as
best to behold all the splendour that shone before
her. On the table were thirteen dishes with gold
and silver covers ; one dish, however, remained un-
disturbed, and was taken away as it was brought on
without anyone having removed the cover. Elspeth
ate of the costly viands, which were nicer than any
cakes she had ever tasted. During the repast there
was much soft talking, but in a language Elspeth

could not understand. The meal ended, the lady
turned and spoke a few words to a maid standing
behind her chair; the maiden hurried from the
room, but soon returned with a little old man,
whose beard was longer than himself. The old
man bowed and remained standing in the doorway.
The lady turned towards him, and pointing to
Elspeth, said :

'Look at that peasant maiden; I wish to adopt
her. Form an imitation of her for me to send into
the village to-morrow to take her place.'

The old man looked keenly at Elspeth, as though
taking her measure, then he bowed to the lady and
withdrew.

The lady now called Elspeth to her, and said
kindly :

'Kiisike has begged me to let you remain here,
and you also expressed a desire to stay. Is this
still your wish?'

Elspeth fell on her knees, and kissed the lady's
hands and feet in her delight at this merciful
deliverance from the clutches of her wicked stepmother.

The lady raised her from the ground, and stroking
her hair and tear-stained cheeks, said :

'If you are tractable and obedient, all will go
well with you; I will care for you, and see you
receive all necessary instruction until you are grown
up, and able to take care of yourself. My maidens
who instruct Kiisike will help you to acquire knowledge, and teach you all kinds of handiwork.'

After a time the old man returned, having a pail

'FORM ME AN IMITATION OF THIS MAIDEN.'

filled with clay on his shoulder, and a small covered
basket in his left hand. Placing these on the ground,
he took a lump of clay and fashioned it into a doll,
with the form of a human being. In the body, that
was hollow, he placed three pickled anchovies, and
a piece of bread. He next made a hole in the doll's
breast, took from the basket a black snake, a yard
long, and made it creep through the hole. The
snake hissed and lashed its tail, as though striving
to resist, but it was compelled to obey. When the
lady had examined the doll, the old man said:

'Nothing now is wanting save a drop of this
peasant child's blood.'

On hearing these words Elspeth turned pale with
terror. But the lady comforted her.

'Fear not, my child!' said she; 'we do not
wish your blood for anything bad, but only for your
future happiness.'

With this she took a small gold needle, pricked
Elspeth's arm with it, and handed it to the old
man, who drove it into the doll's heart. Then he
laid the clay figure into the basket to grow, and
promised to show it to the lady on the following
morning. After this they all retired to rest. Elspeth
was led to a room where a soft bed had been prepared for her.

On awaking the next morning she noticed with
astonishment and delight rich clothes lying on the
chair beside her bed. Presently a servant entered,
told Elspeth to wash and comb her hair, and then
helped her to don the beautiful garments.

Nothing gave the child so much pleasure as the

shoes. Until now she had always gone barefoot. In
Elspeth's opinion a king's daughter could not have
possessed more lovely shoes. In her delight at
these, she paid no heed to the other articles of
clothing, although everything was most beautiful.
Her own clothes had been removed during the
night; wherefore? That she would learn later.
Her clothes had really been put on the doll that
was to personate her in the village. This doll had
grown in the night, and by morning had become an
exact image of Elspeth ; moreover, it walked about
just like a human being.

The poor child was much terrified when she saw
the doll that looked just as she had done the previous day. Noticing her terror, the lady said :

' Do not fear, my child; that clay doll can do you
no harm. We shall send it to your stepmother in
your stead. She may beat it as much as she likes,
the stony-hearted doll can feel no pain ; but, unless
the wicked woman alters her behaviour, there will
come a day when your substitute will award her the
punishment she deserves.' ·

From that day Elspeth lived as happy a life as
child could lead. She knew neither care nor
sorrow ; learning became easier to her each day, and
her former hard life in the village seemed only as an
evil dream. But the deeper she experienced the joy
of this new life, the more wonderful it all appeared.
It could not be brought about by natural means—an
unknown, inexplicable power must govern here. In
the courtyard, about twenty paces from the house,
stood a block of granite. When meal times arrived,

the old man with the long beard approached the
rock, and, drawing a small silver rod from his
bosom, struck the block thrice. Then from the
enormous mass of granite a large golden cock
sprang forth, and stood on the summit of the rock.
As often as the bird crowed and flapped his wings,
something came out of the block. First came a long,
covered table, on which there were as many plates
as there were persons to eat, and this table ran of
itself into the house, as though borne on the wings
of the wind. When the cock crowed a second time,
chairs came forth, and ran after the table ; then the
dishes, with the various meats, one after the other—
all came out from the rock and flew like the wind
to the dining-table. In like manner came flasks
of mead, apples and strawberries. Everything
seemed to be alive, so that none needed to lift or
to carry.

When the meal was ended, the old man went a
second time to the rock and struck it with his silver
wand ; the golden cock crowed, and immediately
flasks, dishes, plates, chairs and table—all disappeared within the rock from whence they had
come. But whenever the thirteenth dish made its
appearance, out of which, by the way, nothing was
ever eaten, a great black cat ran after the dish, and
both cat and dish remained on the block beside the
cock until the old man bore them away. He took
the dish in his hands and the cat in his arms, then,
placing the cock on his shoulder, he disappeared
with them beneath the granite rock. And not only
food and drinks, but all the household necessaries,

and even clothes, came from this wonderful stone at the crowing of the cock.

Although at table little was said, and that always in a strange language that Elspeth could not understand, yet there was much talking and singing when Kiisike's mother walked with her maidens through the rooms or in the grounds. Gradually Elspeth learned to understand the language of her companions, but many years passed ere she could accustom her tongue to form the strange sounds.

Once she asked Kiisike why the thirteenth dish came daily to table, since none ate of it, but Kiisike could not enlighten her. She must, however, have told her mother of the question, for a few days later the lady called Elspeth, and spoke to her earnestly.

'Do not trouble your heart with useless inquiries. You wish to know why we never eat of the thirteenth dish. See, dear child, that is the dish of hidden blessings. We may not touch them, else our happy life here would cease. It would be much better for mankind in the outer world if they did not, in their covetousness, snatch all gifts for themselves, leaving nothing for which to thank the Heavenly Dispenser of Blessings. Covetousness in mankind is a great fault.'

To Elspeth in her happiness the years flew fast. She had grown to maidenhood, and had learned much that in her village home she would not have known all her life long. Kiisike, on the contrary, remained ever the same little child as she was on the day she first met Elspeth in the forest. Every day Elspeth and Kiisike received instruction in read-

ing, writing, and all kinds of fine needlework. Elspeth
learnt everything eagerly, but Kiisike preferred
childish games to useful occupations. If the whim
seized her, she would throw aside her work, seize
her little basket and run into the open air to play
on the sea, and no one thought her wrong in this.
Ofttimes she would say to Elspeth :

' For shame, Elspeth, to grow so big ; you can no
longer play with me.'

Nine years had passed thus, when one evening the
lady called Elspeth into her sleeping chamber. The
maiden wondered at the summons, for, until now,
she had never been allowed to enter it. Her heart
beat wildly. As she crossed the threshold, she
noticed that the lady's cheeks were flushed and her
eyes full of tears, which she hastily brushed aside as
though not wishing them to be seen.

' Dear foster-child,' she began, ' the time has
come when we must part.'

' Part !' cried Elspeth, throwing herself sobbing at
the lady's feet. ' No, dearest lady, that can never be
until death comes to claim one of us. Having once
so kindly received me, do not thrust me from you !'

But the lady answered soothingly :

' Peace, my child ! You do not understand.
What I do is done for your happiness. You are
grown up now, and I dare no longer keep you here.
You must go once more amongst mankind, where
much happiness awaits you.'

Elspeth begged piteously :

' Dearest, dearest lady, cast me not away ! I
desire no other happiness than to live with you, and

with you to die. Make me one of your maids, or
give me any other work—do with me as you please,
but do not send me forth into the pitiless world.
It had been better to have left me in the village with
my cruel stepmother than to have kept me for so
many years to drive me forth again into misery.'

' Be still, dear child,' replied the lady, ' you cannot understand that I am compelled to do this for
your happiness, or how much it grieves me to part
with you. But it must be as I say. You are a
mortal, human child, your years in time will come to
an end, therefore it is you can no longer remain
here. I, and those who surround me, have, it is
true, human forms, but we are not human as you
are. We are creatures of a higher and, to you,
incomprehensible nature. You will shortly find a
fond husband, and with him will live in happiness
until your days draw to a close. It will not be easy
to me to part from you, but it must be, therefore you
must submit quietly.'

Saying this, she drew her golden comb through
Elspeth's hair and sent her to bed. But where on
this sad night could poor Elspeth hope to find sleep ?
Her future life rose before her like a dark and star-
less night.

We will now leave Elspeth to indulge her grief,
and, repairing to the village, take a glance at her
father's house, where the clay doll lived in her
stead, the object of all the stepmother's cruelty and
hate. That a wicked woman does not become
better as she grows older is well known. The stepmother tormented the doll day and night, but the

hard creature whose body felt no pain heeded it
not.   Once her husband tried to help the poor
child, but his wife only beat him cruelly for inter-
fering.

One day, after having beaten the child more
cruelly than usual, she threatened to kill her.
Raging, she seized the doll with both hands round
the throat, and tried to strangle her.   Immediately
a black snake came hissing out of the child's mouth,
and stung the stepmother's tongue, so that she fell
back dead.   When the husband returned home in
the evening he found his wife lying dead on the
floor, but the child was nowhere to be found.

His cries brought in the villagers.   The neigh-
bours said that about dinner-time they had heard a
great noise in the house, but as this was of almost
daily occurrence, no one heeded it.   In the after-
noon all had been quiet, but the daughter had not
been seen.   The body of the dead woman was then
washed and clothed, and herbs and salt cooked for
those who were to watch the dead.

The tired husband went to his chamber to rest,
sincerely thankful that he was at length rid of this
firebrand.   On the table lay three pickled anchovies
and a piece of bread ; he ate them, and then lay
down to sleep.   The next morning he was found
dead in his bed.   A few days later husband and
wife were laid in the same grave, and could do no
further harm.   The peasants never heard anything
of the daughter who had so strangely disappeared.

Poor Elspeth did not close her eyes the whole
night, but wept without ceasing, and bemoaned the

cruel fate that compelled her to part from all those she loved. In the morning the lady placed a signet ring on her finger, and hung a small gold box round her neck. Then she summoned the old man, pointed to Elspeth, and took leave of the maiden with sorrowful mien.

Elspeth was about to thank her kind benefactress, when the old man softly touched her head thrice with his silver wand. Immediately she felt herself change to a bird ; her arms became wings, her legs eagle's feet with long talons, her nose changed to a crooked beak, and feathers covered her body. Then she rose into the air, and soared away amid the clouds, just like an eagle hatched from an egg. She flew southwards many days, resting at times when her wings were tired, but never feeling hungry.

It happened one day that she soared across a lonely forest where hunting dogs barked at her, but these, having no wings, could not harm the bird. Suddenly a sharp arrow pierced her feathers, and she fell to the ground, where she lay senseless through fright.

When she awoke from her swoon and looked around, she was lying beneath a thicket in human form. How she came thither, and all the strange things that had happened, lay behind her like a dream. Then a noble young prince rode up, sprang from his horse, and, kindly offering her his hand, said :

'In a happy hour I rode forth this morning. Dearest maiden, I have dreamt of you every night for half a year, and also that I should find you in this forest; but although I have passed this way in vain a hundred times, my longing and my hope never failed. To-day I shot a large eagle—it must have fallen about here. I came to seek it, and found instead of an eagle—you, my beloved!'

Then he helped Elspeth on his horse, and rode with her to the town, where the old king received her with joy. A few days later a magnificent wedding was celebrated; on the wedding morning Elspeth's kind foster-mother sent her fifty cart-loads of costly presents. After the old king's death Elspeth became queen, and in her old age related the history of her youth. But since then no one has seen or heard anything of the Tontla Forest.

THE END